# KISSES ON MY NECK

*The romantic and sensual love story between two strangers.*

# CHAPTER 1

**Jane** shivered as she spotted one of the numerous bunnies that plagued the city. The bunnies continued to remain around despite the conclusion of the spring holiday and celebrations; they had been for well over a year. It appeared that her city's growth and restoration to greatness took one step forward and two steps back.

The fingers of the elves  warlock twitched as she weaved spells, and then a gigantic ball of green bale-fire erupted from her own fingertips. The rabbit was instantly destroyed, just a husk remaining. Jane continued on smiling after being satisfied.


She was dressed in her go-to outfit, an exotic dress with an exotic foreign design and the most exposed V-shaped bodice of any dress in the land. She was able to display the intricately adorned ruby necklace and the fine, delicate swirls of gold

wire that were used to make it. She had modest

breasts with a beautiful round cleavage and

flawless light ivory skin, and the gorgeous jewelry

fit perfectly between them. Jane strolled with her

hips gently swaying, which she knew attracted the

attention of several guards she passed. Well-

trained, they didn't dare turn to look as she passed

them.

However, the glances she received as she approached them always gave her the shivers. Oh, how she wished she could taint one of them. That would be very enjoyable.

The next guard to pass, Jane grinned as she observed his eyes were not on her but rather behind her. to the side of her. The guard's eyes sharpened, and she caught sight of him nodding as he moved within her line of sight.

Behind her, someone was. Also awfully near, almost too close. She dared to take a self-portrait as she turned to proceed into one of the city's connecting passageways, a dimly lit, dimly lit tunnel full of dark corners.

As youthful as she seemed to most others, he was also young. As Jane went into the brightness of the following area of the city, she turned her head back around and grinned. The man had long, black hair, and he was dressed in scarlet. His

pantaloons were slack about the thighs but fitted

snugly around his boots.

Why was he so close and who was he?

She noticed another rabbit as she was passing the

ranger training grounds. A man was only a few

feet behind her, and she could feel his gaze

burning into her rear. Jane grinned as she twitched

her fingers and fired another rabbit, this time

barely missing the target since she knew she was

being watched. Before throwing itself upward in

anguish and landing on its back on the burnt grass,

the creature let out a terrible squeal. The warlock

approached to closely examine her work and

prodded the creature with her toe.


A man's voice virtually whispered in her ear,

"Poor bunny." You've obliterated him,

She lowered herself to the rabbit's carcass and

drew out a finely designed knife before

whispering back, "Slippers."

"Slippers?"

"Yes. He'll make the ideal footwear."

As the woman flipped the rabbit onto its side, there was a faint mocking chuckle from behind her. You should hire a leather-worker for that, right?

Jane grinned, responding less verbally and more physically. She smiled as she parted the rabbit's half-soft, half-crisp hide from its body, rolled the hide's bloody side down into a tube, and tucked it into a bag at her hip. Then she made some cuts in

the sinewy tendons that she would later save and

cure into rope or "thread" for the clothing she

would later sew.

"I believe I've got that covered,"

Jane sheathed her knife once more after wiping it

on the leaves of a nearby plant and standing up.

She turned to walk away after using more leaves

to clean her long fingers of blood and gore. The

man went after. She sensed his presence. And it

was exhilarating. Dangerous. Also, good.

The man proceeded to follow her and said, "That

is quite some skill you have.

What about a pair of slippers?

Why, I would, you ask. The concept almost had

the man excited.


Jane gurgled, not looking back as she replied,

"Good." "I'll hide them under my bed for you."


The man sat quiet for a long time, not

understanding what she was implying. Jane

almost believed he had gone, but she could still

feel his presence following her.

But I don't know where your bed is, he said softly, altering his tone just enough to reveal what he had understood from her comments.

She smiled and replied, "I guess you have a problem then." She then made her way up a protracted, winding ramp toward the court and throne room of the rulers of her people.

They had to past numerous guards, but the man followed closely still. By this point, everyone who saw them could feel their contentment and that they were "together." No woman would allow a

stranger to follow them so closely without tensing

up her own step. Jane was also at ease. They

avoided the main area where political leaders

deliberated the course of the race by moving

through the courts instead. When Jane touched the

light sphere that she had guided them both to, the

man's hand was virtually in her own.

As she was carried through the orb's potent portal

to the realms beyond, which belonged to the

living allies of the elves, she felt his breath on her

neck.

Jane waited for the man while smoothing her

dress. She didn't look up and pretended to be

interested in her outfit despite the shimmering air

in front of her. Her hands were moving across her

bodice's V cut like white butterflies, dragging it in

different directions while pretending to adjust.

She was aware that the man was forced to observe

what she was doing with his gaze as he turned to

face her.


Before squeezing the dress tighter, she

purposefully sank her fingers into the V cut's

margins, almost revealing the darker rose hue of

her nipples in the process. She then walked past

the ruins and towards the heart of the city while

pivoting on her heel.

The man said over one of her shoulders, "That...is

a very nice outfit.

Jane's chin rose as she smiled cockily and replied,

"Yes, I understand. It enables me to display my

heirloom jewelry.

In his reply, the man's sardonic smirk could be

heard. "True. Your jewelry is absolutely stunning.

But..."

The man abruptly stopped so he was immediately

behind her after almost colliding with her as she

hesitated in her step. The thick embroidered

material on the dress' back allowed her to feel his

heat on her.


But your hairstyle," the stranger muttered. Jane

felt her breath stop in her throat as she suspected

he could be caressing her hair.

"Your hair obscures my view of your gorgeous

neck,"

It does? she questioned in a trembling voice,

swallowing as she felt the tip of his finger brush

across the skin of her neck.

"Yes. Your neck would be considerably more

kissable if you had a different hairstyle."

Jane slowly extended her hand to the side. "I'll

change my hair if you have the money to pay for

it."


She naturally possessed a covertly submissive

side to the warlock's generally powerful

personality. Under the correct circumstances, even

the simplest commands may be carried out. She

enjoyed obeying a stranger in this manner. She

resumed her stroll once he gave her the right

quantity of coins in her hand.

She asked without turning back, "Coming?"

Where are we headed?

Jane shook her head and grinned slightly. "Of

course, to the barber."

As they made their way deeper into the

underground metropolis that the abandoned living

of this region called home, neither of them spoke.

For whatever reason, a goblin had established a

barbershop here. Everyone knew the dead had

very little hair left and that little they did have was

in danger of falling out, so it was foolish of him to

act in this way. A more shrewd goblin would have

opened shop in the elf city, where there would

have been more customers and a market that

would have been far more receptive to such a

pointless service.

Jane sat down in the barber's chair and ignored the

goblin's jokes about being happy to have actual

clients. He undoubtedly fought to get them to sit

in this identical chair throughout the day after

seeing their leathery, sunken looks all day. Jane

could tell he was happy to have such a lovely

customer, but when he reached out to touch the

horns that protruded from her forehead and were

encrusted with gems, she fended off his rapacious

hands.

The majority of folks didn't care to notice her

horns. She liked it more that way. The ones who

did were simply casually bringing them up

because they wanted to engage her in

conversation rather than out of dread. That

happened to her more than once, particularly in

the orc capital. However, such inquiries might be

quickly put to rest with a quick chuckle and touch

of her jewelry. All eyes would be drawn to the

woman's gleaming white cleavage from the

unusual, probably ornamental horns by the rubies

that nestled so prettily on her breasts.

When the goblin was finished, Jane carefully got

up from the chair and turned to look in the mirror.

Once again facing the man who had followed her

all the way here, she then turned around. He lifted

himself up from leaning against the stone wall and

stood staring at her as she moved to stand close to him.

She raised an eyebrow and gently replied, "Well. "Not my preferred hairdo. But there is a need for it..."

Her long, dark hair had been styled into a silly-looking coil atop her head that resembled a woven cornucopia or horn-shaped basket. The remainder of her hair was pulled back and gave the horrible coil an ugly tail by being gathered at the nape of her neck and brushed up and back. But the result was that her neck was now completely exposed.

Jane carefully positioned her hands behind her and leaned back against the same wall as the other elf was. He walked up to her with ease and placed one hand at her hip and the other against the wall close to her face.

He kissed her lips, saying softly, "It's beautiful."

Jane promptly made a U-turn. She hadn't done this for mouth-to-mouth kissing; she had done it for other purposes. Slowly returning her gaze to the man, she seriously blinked at him. He acknowledged her point and nodded in agreement.

The man's mouth shifted to her neck, and she groaned quietly. His delicate, sucking kisses on her alabaster skin caused her to shiver all over as he continued to kiss her there. Nearly in the open, they were. The barber was gawking at the two

elves while he cleaned his scissors and other tools

in full view of the public.

Jane grinned and tilted her head in the direction of

one of the mirrors while keeping her eyes open.

She could now both see and feel the man

consuming her neck. Slowly rising and inexorably

advancing toward the cut in her dress was the

hand at her hip. He avoided the untied strings

there—useless laces that were almost ever

fastened. She gasped as he grabbed one of her breasts as his hand began to move deeper into the fabric. But she kept her hands behind her the entire time, picturing them being bound and fastened there.

Her chest rose and sank as the stranger gripped her round tit, squeezed it, and pushed it clear of her dress so that even the goblin could see as he pinched and strained at the dark nipple. She was forced to breathe more forcefully. Her areola contracted, and the stranger repeatedly tugged, pinched, and rolled her nipple until it was a stiff little bud. Jane cried out in hunger and slid up and down against the wall.

He was aware of it. He finally pulled the dress off of one shoulder and nipped at the exposed curve of flesh since he knew his prey well. When he abruptly twisted Jane around, she barely avoided having her face rubbed on the rough stone by pressing her hands up against the wall in time.

As he pulled her dress up the back of her legs, the

man hissed in her ear. His fingers were drawn to

her hips, and she could sense that he assumed she

was wearing some form of pantyhose. Not at all.

Jane's tight little bottom was pinched by the

stranger, who grunted loudly and with much

enjoyment. This caused her white flesh to turn

crimson.

The goblin's mouth was open, and his jaw was

limp. He was no longer cleaning anything.

However,Jane mostly kept her gaze fixed on the

mirror while the man behind her struggled to

separate his leggings. She observed her mirror as

the stranger prodded her pussy behind with the

large head and then dragged his dick up and down

the cleft of her ass. He pulled her lower body

away from the wall by applying pressure on her

shoulders and grabbing one of her hips. Then, he

took a large step between her feet before striking

her forcefully.

Now that his teeth were uncomfortably hard on

her neck, Jane could feel them. He would sever

his teeth and spit blood.  She urgently wanted him

to, so she bit her lower lip. She kept her eyes open,

observing her own face in the mirror, despite how

his fucking and biting made her grimace.

Her body was now being pulled back and forth by

the man as he reached down with both hands,

pushing her tight, small cunt to glide quickly over

his long, veined shaft. Guards passed the

barbershop as they walked by, but none stopped to

peek inside to see the filthy goblin whom

everyone detested. He was currently thankful that

they never peeked inside at him. He would have

hated for the performance he was seeing to end.

When Jane realized how much of herself was on display for the goblin barber, she couldn't help but smile. It increased the excitement of the situation overall.

She gasped as she sensed the man getting bigger. He would soon arrive. The guy proceeded to kick Jane in the ass with his hips and groin, reaching around to the front of her body with his hands. As he fucked into her hole, one hand stretched down and gripped her pubis in a possessive manner. The fingers dipped in and out, wriggled over her

clitoris, and teased at her labia. Her dress was torn

from one breast by the other hand, which then

started to care for both of them expertly and

viciously. Her nipples hurt, the sensation acute

and agonizing at the same time.


As she flattened her cheek against the stone and

felt sweat start to appear on her forehead, her

fingers began to curl into claw shapes.

Jane arrived at the same time as the visitor. More

from the desire for what they were doing than

from the sensation of him erupting deep inside her

womb. Fucking in front of complete strangers in a

random barbershop with a goblin hairdresser

acting as their spectator and watcher. She could

see in the mirror that it was still pouring the

mixture of their juices as the stranger drew his

cock out from in between her thighs. She

observed him examining it with his thumb

running over it.

Then he stroked her anus with the wet pad of that same thumb. She yelled in pain when he shoved his thumb into her ass and went limp at the intrusive, filthy touch. Before moving it, the man held his thumb still for a moment.

He labored to pull up his leggings as he slowly withdrew his thumb. While attempting to catch her breath again, Jane panted heavily while grinning at herself in the mirror. The goblin kept staring, but this time he was wiping his scissors for the hundredth time. Jane was given permission to turn around once the stranger took a step back.

She said, leaning back against the wall for support, "I have to go. The man's expression of dismay was the cherry on top of a delicious and cunning cake for Lilith.

He attempted a grin and continued, "I want to see you again."

She muttered, hands fiddling with her dress, "If

you're nearby."


You owe me slippers, I say.


Jane gave him a cheek pat while grinning. They'll

be in my bed, I said.

She then sashayed off, trying her best to appear

graceful despite the fact that her cunt hurt like

she'd been punched by a bovine.

She could hear the other person saying, "But...but

I don't know where you live," as she turned to go.

Jane waved to the man standing behind her, but

she didn't even turn around to give him a grin

before vanishing into the shadows of the city.